CHAPTER ONE

The pain hits me before I can even open my eyes. I try to move, but my entire body feels like I've been run over by a semi-truck. I put my hand on my head to feel where the throbbing is coming from. I feel a fresh wound and hiss when I touch it. I finally open my eyes to check my hand for blood. My fingertips are streaked with the dark red liquid, but nothing too serious.

I try to adjust my eyes to the light before looking around. I don't recognize the room and I start to freak out instantly. I attempt to sit up hurriedly, but my body is too sore for me to make any sudden movements. I raise up slightly, noticing my black yoga pants and pink sports bra that I had on during my workout. I retrace my steps in my mind quickly, realizing that my last memory was of me leaving the gym. I remember parking around the corner because I wanted to get my steps up, but I don't ever recall making it back to my car.

I sit up a little more and see the chain around my leg. My eyes get big once I notice the other end of the chain disappearing into a dark red, velvet wall. I grunt my way up into a fully seated position and reach for the ankle restraint. The metal is cold, thick and it won't budge. *I'm trapped.*

I finally look around the room, noticing several other women laid out randomly on the floor of the huge space. They are all dressed differently and I don't recognize any of them. I try to shout to wake them up but no one stirs from their slumber. I let out a frustrated noise before yanking at the chain around my leg again. I notice the lock on the side of the ankle brace and reach for the pin in my hair. Part of my bun falls as I try to pick the lock like I see people attempt in the movies.

"What the fuck?" Another lady finally wakes up and I look over at her. She's the furthest from me in the room so I can't fully see her face.

"Hey! Hey, you! Are you chained up?" Silence lingers for a second before the lady finally speaks again.

"Chained up? What the fuck are you talking about?!" She sits up and I can finally see her clearly. She's a fair-skinned, 30-something years old woman with dark brown hair. It looks like it used to be up in a neat french roll, but now it's flopping all over the place. She wears a black evening gown that looks like it cost more than my car. Her cheeks are stained with mascara as if she were crying not too long ago. Her eyes meet mine and we stare at each other. She tries to stand up but winces in pain.

"Ahh! Ssss! What the hell?!" She lifts up her dress to reveal a bluish purple bruise covering half of her leg. She notices the chain around her ankle immediately afterward and gets hysterical. "Oh my God! Oh my fucking God! What the fuck is going on here?! Why am I chained up?!" She tugs at the chain angrily and yells loudly. She screams so loudly that another woman opens her eyes.

"Wha-" she says, unable to get an entire word out. She looks around the room and sits up quickly. "What-where am I?!" Her blue eyes get big as they land on her chained up leg. She wildly tries to get free, causing her floral nightgown to fly up and reveal her white underwear. She kicks around like a captured animal until she finally gets tired.

One by one, the remaining six women wake up from their slumber. Some have bruises, some have fresh wounds, some aren't hurt at all, but all have chains around their legs. Everyone is so distraught in their own minds that no one has yet attempted to figure out what's going on here. I shout for them to calm down after realizing that I can't bear to listen to one more woman ask where she is. They all get quiet and look at my brown face and I clear my throat.

"Us yelling and crying won't get us out of here! We have to try to figure out what's going on and who's doing this to us!" They all look at me like I'm speaking a foreign language and I sigh. "Can any of you at least remember anything that happened before you ended up here? Like someone drugging you, hitting you, dragging you away?" They all look around at each other before thinking to themselves. A young woman that barely looks 18 speaks up first.

"Well, I was babysitting for the Turners, and once they arrived back home, I left to walk around the corner to my house. I don't remember how far I got, but evidently I didn't make it."

"Yeah, same here." A heavy-set woman in dark jeans and a yellow t-shirt chimes in, "I wasn't babysitting, but I did just drop my two boys off at the daycare. I had errands to run but I don't remember making it to the car after I left the post office."

"Oh my God, this is fucking nuts," the lady in the expensive gown adds, "I was at an art exhibit with my husband when I stepped away to use the facilities. I stepped into a stall and that's all I remember." She looks at me with a puzzled expression and everyone looks at each other the same way. I close my eyes to search my memory to see if I could recall a mysterious character, but I quickly draw a blank.

"Hey, does anyone remember seeing anyone mysterious or suspicious? Did anything out of the ordinary happen right before your last memory?" All the women begin to think again before shaking their heads no. The lady wearing the floral nightgown has an 'ah ha' moment as her eyes widen.

"Hey! I remember something! I didn't think it was anything at the time, but now that I think about it, it probably has something to do with this." She stops talking as if she's trying to get her thoughts in order. We all wait impatiently for her to continue, "I stay with my parents, but they haven't been home in almost a week. They are away on a cruise for their anniversary. But anyway, I hardly leave the house anymore, so I thought it was strange when I noticed that my house keys had been moved. Like, I keep them near the front door on a hook but last night, they were sitting on the foyer table. I figured that maybe they fell off of the hook and landed there, but now that I think about it, that makes no sense at all. The table is a few feet away from the hook, so if they would have fallen, they would have hit the floor." Everyone stares at her quietly as fear starts to cover their faces. The woman wearing the evening gown changes her sitting position, being careful not to aggravate her bruised leg.

"Now that you mention it, something subtle like that happened to me, too." Everyone turns to look at her as she fixes the bottom of her dress, "My husband couldn't pick me up for the exhibit, so he sent one of his drivers. The guy showed up in an outdated limo and didn't even open the door for me. So, eventually, I got in the car myself and started cursing at his discourteous ass, and do you know what he did? He rolled up the partition on me!" I make a face at her and shake my head. *This lady can't be serious.* "So, we arrived at the gallery and as you can guess, he didn't open the door for me again. I jumped out angrily and the guy just sped off. I went inside to find my husband

and I told him that I wanted that driver fired immediately.

He looked at me weirdly, like he didn't know what I was

talking about, and then he said, "I just talked to my driver

two minutes ago, he's still at the house waiting for you to

come out"."

CHAPTER TWO

We all sit in silence again as chills form up and down my

arms. Whoever is doing this seems to be incredibly

organized and methodical.

"Well, did you see his face?" I ask the lady wearing

the dress and she shakes her head no.

"Not at all. He never got out of the car and he rolled the partition up so quickly that I couldn't even make out a single feature. Hell, I can't even say for sure if it were a man or not." We get quiet again and I look around at everyone's frightened faces. I look at how different we all are and shake my head. *We don't seem to have anything obvious in common, so it has to be a deeper reason to why we're here.*

"So, I've been thinking. This has to be some sort of game or test or something. Like, why else would we all be here chained up like this with each other?" the lady with the nightgown on throws out. A woman wearing all black smacks her lips at her suggestion.

"A fucking game? What the fuck is this supposed to be, the movie *Saw* or something? You're a stupid fucking cunt!" She shouts at her and I intervene.

"Hey, that's totally uncalled for. Especially when no one else is coming up with any bright ideas." The goth looking chick turns her attention towards me.

"You know what, I'm getting really tired of hearing your voice. Who the fuck voted you kidnapper's captain?" I sigh loudly. She is going to make this situation much more unpleasant than it already is. I decide to ignore her.

"Hey, what's your name?" I ask the woman in the night clothes. She glances at Ms. Goth before answering my question.

"I'm Linda."

"Hey Linda, my name is Jessica." I throw her a fake smile and she does the same, "Now, what were you saying?" She takes a deep breath before she responds.

"I was saying how this could be some sort of test or something. Like, if this person wanted to kill us, then we'd already be dead. And if this person was a rapist, then we all wouldn't be in the same room like this. We're not wearing any gags or anything, so we're meant to talk to each other. I think we're supposed to figure something out." Everyone looks at her as they try to register what she's saying. I stare at her, too, realizing that she has a point.

"Well, if that's true, then we should start talking this thing out and try to figure out what we all have in common," the woman in the ball gown suggests. She looks at all of our faces, "My name is Brandi. Brandi Fonzarelli."

"Fonzarelli? Like the hotel chain?" The lady in the yellow shirt asks.

"Yeah, that's the one. Gene Fonzarelli is my husband." Everyone makes a surprised face.

"Oh wow. No disrespect honey, but those hotels have been around longer than you've been alive. My parents used to stay there all of the time," the woman in yellow adds. Brandi smirks and looks at her wedding ring.

"I know. My husband is 40 years older than me."

We gasp and the goth chick laughs.

"Ok, so we know her story now, she's a gold digger. Who's next?" Brandi rolls her eyes at the goth female's accusations before looking in her direction. She grins before acknowledging her.

"Well, since you have so much to say, you're next. What's your story, sweetie? You got kidnapped after leaving the meth lab or something?" Goth girl puts her middle finger up at Brandi, revealing her chipped, black nail polish. We all stare at her waiting for her to answer. She looks down awkwardly before speaking.

"Well, if you must know, my name is CeCe, and I can't remember what I was doing before all of this happened." She looks away from us nervously as if she's lying and I raise an eyebrow. She starts fiddling with her nail polish before the lady in yellow chimes in.

"I told everyone what I remembered, and my name is Cynthia," she gets emotional all of a sudden, "And I just want to get out of here! I'm the only person that my kids can depend on so who's going to take care of them if I'm not there?!" She begins to sob loudly and my heart breaks for her. I can't imagine the pain she's going through. *I don't have any kids*.

The woman sitting closest to her tries to slide over and console her but is unable to get to her. She gets frustrated and gives up as I realize that we haven't heard from her yet.

"Hey, hey you?" She looks in my direction, "We haven't heard anything from you yet. What's your name?" She stares at me for a second before looking at everyone else. She starts doing sign language and I instantly get confused.

"She's saying that her name is Sam and that she hasn't said a word since she woke up from her coma over a year ago." The babysitter translates for Sam and Sam thanks her.

"Wow, you know sign language?" The babysitter grins at my question.

"Yeah, I take an ASL class at Smith University."

"Wow, Smith U. I heard that's a great school, but hard to get in, though. Are you doing classes online or something?"

"No. I'm a campus student." I look at her strangely.

"Oh, so you must be on break then." She returns the same look to me.

"No. I just had class yesterday before I went to my babysitting gig." I make a puzzled face before responding.

"We must not be talking about the same Smith University, then. The one I'm referring to is in Florida."

"Yeah..." She nods her head at me as if she's trying to figure out what I'm getting at.

"Well, that's impossible. We're not in Florida, we're in Michigan."

"Michigan?" Brandi speaks up, "No, we're in California."

"Wait a minute, you all are wrong. I just dropped my kids off a few hours ago, and we stay in Maine."

"No, no, no," Linda shakes her head, "I just went to bed in Utah." We all look at each other with horrified expressions as CeCe starts to laugh again.

"Well, look at that. I guess we're not in Kansas anymore, Toto."

CHAPTER THREE

Everyone starts chattering hysterically at the same time and I close my eyes. I breathe deeply, trying to stop my anxiety from taking over my body. It seems like the more we talk, the more confusing things get. *There has to be a reason behind all of this madness!*

"Who has the power to do this?" Linda asks, placing her knees up and covering them with her nightgown. She hugs her legs and begins to rock swiftly.

"The government," a new voice says, and we all look in the direction of it. An Asian woman holds her lower back as she fixes her position. "I've been on the government's tail for a while now. You wouldn't believe all of the heinous shit they're responsible for. They do experiments on people just because they feel like it. We're nothing but lab rats to them. I'm sure this is just another one of their sick tests." She looks around the room curiously and another new voice laughs.

"Of course Amy Wong would say that." We divert our attention to another overlooked face and she shakes her head.

"Wait a minute, you two know each other?" I ask the blonde-haired woman and she sighs.

"Yeah… unfortunately," she runs her fingers through her short cut, "And let her tell it, everything that happens is a conspiracy or because of 'the man'. She's obsessed with ridiculous shit like that."

"Ridiculous? That's funny. You didn't think it was so ridiculous when you were the lead blogger on my website." The blonde-haired female smacks her lips at Amy's words before CeCe interrupts them.

"Wait a fucking minute, how is it that you two are the only people in here that seem to know each other? How the fuck did that happen?" I glance at CeCe and then back at the women. *That is a good question.*

"I have no fucking idea. Let's ask the conspiracy theorist over there to explain that. Let me guess, it was the aliens that the government is covering up, right? Or is it the pharmaceutical company using us as test dummies for their new drugs?" Amy narrows her eyes at her and grinds her teeth.

"You know what Kimberly, you're a real piece of shit! After everything we've been through together, you allowed some prick to come into our life and change your mind about me in the snap of a finger-"

"Because he made a lot of sense!"

"And I didn't?!" The ladies abruptly change the subject suddenly and we all get uncomfortable. I don't know what happened between them, but evidently, it's unresolved. The ladies stop arguing and everything gets awkwardly quiet. Linda looks at Amy before speaking.

"You said you think the government is behind this - why do you think that?" CeCe laughs at Linda's question but both women ignore her.

"Because, look at how everything was done. Whoever kidnapped us knew a lot about us, down to our habitual actions and even our plans for the evening," she glances at Brandi, "They were able to infiltrate our lives without anything more than a subtle eyebrow raise or two. Plus, we have no idea where we are, and contrary to what you all may think, you have no idea how much time has passed. Some of you think it's the same day you were abducted, or the next day even, but in all actuality, we really have no fucking idea how long it's been. All that we know is that we were meant to wake up at the same time so that we can begin to work through whatever the hell is going on here." Everyone stares at her as if she's giving a lecture. Her face goes from serious to fearful before she continues, "I looked around and I don't see anywhere for us to go to the bathroom or any signs that we'll be fed," she swallows hard, "So that means that A. We're on a time limit to figure out whatever it is we need to figure out, or B. We won't be alive long enough to need food, water or a toilet."

CHAPTER FOUR

We all look around the room and realize that she's right. There's nothing else in here besides us and the chains around our ankles.The chains disappear into the velvet coverings acting as walls and we have no idea what's on the other side of them. She gets quiet to let the information she provided sink in.

" I have to get the hell out of here!" Linda screams before standing to her feet suddenly and hopping around. She tugs at the chain with her body weight, but it doesn't budge from the wall. We watch her as she makes a pathetic effort to get away. She tries to yank her foot from the chain with all of her might. We see her struggle for a few more seconds until the unthinkable happens. Linda's chain jerks suddenly and she falls and hits her head. She lays there unconscious and many of us start to scream. Her nightgown slides up her hips as her limp body slides across the concrete, red floor.

"Oh my God!" Cynthia yells out as Linda's body gets dangerously close to disappearing under the velvet drapes. Her body stops moving within inches of the covering. My eyes get big once I notice the blood trail that came from her head. I want to vomit, but my stomach is too empty to do so.

"What in the fuck just happened?!" Brandi yells out with a voice as shaky as her body.

"Well, one thing's for certain, these people definitely don't like it when you try to get away." Amy adds with a shaky voice as well. I stare at Linda's lifeless body while feeling so helpless. I don't know if she's dead or alive but I do know one thing, she's in desperate need of medical attention.

"Is she dead?" the babysitter asks with tears running down her face.

"No, but she will be soon if she continues to bleed out like that. I've saw it happen before." CeCe speaks up and we all look at her.

"You've seen what happened before?" Brandi asks her. CeCe looks as if she regrets even bringing it up. She sighs loudly before she answers.

"I've seen someone bleed out from their head before." Shock covers my face.

"So, you've seen someone die?" I ask CeCe.

"Did you murder them?" Brandi overlaps my question with her own and CeCe smacks her lips at her.

"No, I didn't fucking murder him, you gold-digging whore. My best friend and I got into a car accident and his head hit the windshield. The top part of his skull went through it and the glass cut him so badly that he bled out quickly. I wore my seatbelt so I was fine, but I had to watch him die because I was stuck inside of the car with him. He stared at me the entire time he bled out, too. I saw the exact moment that his soul left his body. His eyes went from scared to cold. That was some freaky shit. I still can't erase that image out of my mind." We stare at her with weirded out looks on our faces. We look more bothered than her about her story and I get confused. *I couldn't imagine having to watch my friend die. I'd be in a padded white room for the rest of my life.*

"Her story raises an interesting question. Is there anyone else in this room that's seen someone die?" Amy asks the group and I shake my head no quickly. *I don't handle death well. I've never even been to a funeral.*

Sam raises her hand slowly and I look at her. She makes a face as if the memory still brings her great pain. She stares at the babysitter and the babysitter begins to talk to her with her hands. Sam says something back and the babysitter acknowledges the group.

"I told her that my name was Vicki and asked if she would allow me to translate her story for her. She said she didn't mind." Vicki looks at Sam and Sam continues signing, "She says that the incident that led up to her coma was one filled with death." She pauses to read Sam's hands, "She says that she lives in Colorado, and she was in a small cabin on the mountains when an avalanche fell and snow covered the place completely. Her and her cabin mates were trapped for weeks, and by the time the rescue team reached them, everyone had died but her." I look at Sam with my face covered in sorrow, "The three others had fallen ill from eating some bad food that she didn't eat. She watched them all suffer and die. She sat there with their bodies for two days until she was saved. She says she'll never forget that smell." Most of us make distraught faces as tears surface in Sam's eyes. You can tell the pain is still unbearable for her. "She doesn't remember the rescue team showing up and breaking down the cabin door. She had almost died herself from the lack of food and water. She says she woke up in the hospital a week later and she couldn't talk. She doesn't know why because she could talk just fine before everything happened."

"Something similar to that happened to my little brother. He suffered a traumatic experience when he was five and he didn't speak again until he was about eight." Kimberly piggybacks off of Sam's story and we glance at her. I shake my head slightly as if I agree. *I've heard of that happening before but I never knew anyone that it personally happened to.* Sam begins signing again.

"She says that her therapist said something similar to that but it's very rare that it happens in adults. Most of the time, it's not that the child can't speak, it's that they don't want to speak. She says that she wants to speak so badly, but every time she attempts to do so, her throat closes up and no sound comes out. She says she can't make any type of noises, not even when she cries."

Cynthia shakes her head with pity, "You poor thing." Sam lowers her head and cries inaudibly. The rest of us fight back our own tears as everything gets quiet once more.

"This isn't working." Brandi breaks the silence a few moments later with a frustrated voice, "We've been talking, but we aren't getting anywhere. And poor Linda…" she glances at Linda's motionless body, "We all will end up just like her if we don't find a way out of here!" Brandi almost loses it, but she catches herself before she does. She takes a deep breath and closes her eyes.

"Well, that's because we aren't talking about the right things." Amy speaks and I glance at her, "We are here for a reason, and the more we beat around the bush, the

worse things will be for us. The government is always

watching, and we must've offended them in a serious way.

I think the only way for us to get out of here is to confess.

Confess what we've all done to land us in a situation like

this."

CHAPTER FIVE

Amy takes her time and stares at each one of us. I turn my head when her eyes meet mine. *Even though I'm not a bad person, there was that one time…*

"What?! That's completely fucking ridiculous! We're not here because of the bad shit we've done!" Kimberly yells at Amy and Amy shakes her head at her.

"The first to disagree is always the guiltiest." Kimberly smacks her lips at Amy's comment, but doesn't deny her accusation. The room gets eerily quiet again. Even though we all heard what Amy said, none of us seem to be willing to jump out there first and expose ourselves. *Evidently, keeping our embarrassing business to ourselves is worth dying for.*

"Well, I guess someone needs to open the floor up so… here it goes." We all look in the direction of Vicki as she stares at the ground. She takes a deep breath before she continues, "Well, I… I've been sort of…" she clears her throat, "That family I was telling you about, the Turners, well, I've been sleeping with Mr. Turner." Everyone's mouth falls open as if a cheating husband is so rare and unbelievable. She finally lifts her head and Cynthia gives her a nasty look.

"Ugh! You know, it's folks like you that break up happy homes." Vicki stares at Cynthia for a second before turning away shamefully. CeCe smacks her lips at Cynthia.

"Folks like her? That's fucking bullshit! She's not married to Mrs. Turner so she doesn't owe her shit! It's her husband's job to love, honor, and obey! The only person that can break up his 'happy home' is him!" CeCe takes up for Vicki expeditiously. Cynthia cuts her eyes at her.

"I'm not surprised to hear that coming from you! You have crack whore written all over you! You don't care who you fuck, do you? As long as you can get your drugs, right?" Cynthia's voice gets nastier and CeCe gets offended. I decide to intervene to try to bring the tension down a few notches.

"Cynthia, why did Vicki's confession ruffle your feathers so badly?" She looks at me with an expression so bothered that you would've thought that Mr. Turner was her husband.

"Because! Wives have it hard! We have to work, take care of the kids, cook, clean, and take care of our husbands! Then, these lil' hot in the tail ass girls come around and throw themselves at them like they have no home training! Next thing you know, your husband is leaving you for a slut half your age and you're stuck being a single mom and paying for a mortgage that you can't afford!" She speaks very emotionally, making it evident that she just described what happened in her household. She breathes heavily before tears finally run down her face.

Vicki looks so regretful for bringing up the sore subject that she tucks her face in her hands.

"Hey! The idea was not to attack each other simply because you disagree! Vicki found the courage to put herself out there and be vulnerable in front of us. We can't judge anyone here! Especially when we have yet to confess our own wrongdoings!" Amy says sternly.

"Amen, sister! I know that's right!" Brandi cosigns with a smirk. "I wouldn't be happily married now if I didn't take my husband from his ex-wife." Brandi speaks like she's proud of herself and I shake my head at her. "Don't get mad at the other woman because you couldn't keep your husband at home. Instead of worrying about what she did to get him, try to figure out what you did to lose him. I'm telling you honey, if you redirect some of that energy you're wasting on him and her to the betterment of yourself, you'd love yourself more. And then, maybe you would look like something. You may even look good enough to go and steal your husband back." She stares at Cynthia with her words and Cynthia looks appalled. I see this conversation going in the wrong direction so I try to intervene again.

"So Brandi, is that your confession, then? You stealing your husband from his first wife?" She giggles and shakes her head no.

"First of all, she wasn't his first wife, she was his third. And secondly, no, that's not my confession. My confession is actually a lot worse than that." We all stare at her, waiting for her to divulge more information. She looks around at all of us as if she's happy to be getting our attention, "I'm in a serious sexual relationship with my stepson, Mr. Gene Fonzarelli Jr."

***

Shock fills the room quickly. I stare at her as if I don't know how to respond to that. CeCe shakes her head and laughs.

"Well! That's something that I thought I would only see on Pornhub!" She laughs again and Brandi humps her shoulders.

"Hey, it really does happen, and it feels unbelievably amazing!"

"No… no it doesn't! You're just sick and pathetic!" Cynthia spews out more criticizing words and Brandi humps her shoulders again.

"I'm young, beautiful, and filthy fucking rich. Plus, I have great sex because my partner is supposed to be off limits. And look at you. You're overweight, dressed in a stained t-shirt with dingy ass blue jeans on, and your hair looks like you haven't combed in in months. So, who's the real pathetic one here?" Cynthia's face drops and I frown at Brandi. She notices my expression and acknowledges it.

"Jessica, don't look at me like that. She's been asking for it with all of her judgmental comments. She may want to consider judging her gotdamn self."

"Alright Brandi, we've got it, thank you." Amy interrupts. I can tell she's not happy with Brandi's stories, either, but she's trying her best to remain neutral. "Ok, so who's next?" We look around at each other, but no one volunteers. Sam starts waving frantically, capturing our attention immediately.

"Hey, what is it?" Vicki asks, before Sam starts signing quickly. "Wait… Hold on, slow down! You're going too fast!" Sam gets frustrated and starts pointing towards the spot where Linda's body was resting. We all follow her finger and instantly notice what she's so frantic about.

"Oh my God," I say, covering my mouth. We all stare at a huge blood puddle, but Linda's body is nowhere to be found.

CHAPTER SIX

"Where is she? Wh- Where did she go?" Cynthia questions the air. We stare at the spot for a little while longer before turning around to look at each other.

"No one saw anything?!" I ask the group frantically. Everyone shakes their heads no quickly.

"They must have snatched her up while we were talking." Brandi throws out the most likely possibility in a nervous tone.

"But why?! And where did they take her?!" Kimberly inquires, sounding like her emotions are getting the best of her. She gawks at Amy as if she has the answer and Amy humps her shoulders defensively.

"Don't look at me! I've been trying to figure out a way for us to get out of here! I don't want any of us to get hurt!"

"But maybe they only took her because she tried to get away. Maybe the rest of us are safe if we just- ... AHHH!" Vicki gets tugged away in the middle of her statement and we all start to scream. She kicks and yells her way towards the part of the velvet curtain that's harnessing her chain. I cover my mouth and my heart beats swiftly. *I'm about to freak out! What the hell is going on?!*

"Please! No!" Vicki continues to shout until she stops sliding. Her body settles inches away from the velvet drapes, just like Linda's did.

"Vicki! Are you ok?" I yell at her. I'm breathing so hard that I sound like I'm hyperventilating. She lays there and covers her eyes. She starts crying and I do, too. "We're never going to get out of here alive!" I say, officially breaking down. Amy looks at me with terrified eyes, but still tries to hold everything together.

"Hey, it's ok, Jessica. Everything is going to be ok."

"Bullshit!" CeCe shouts out, "It is NOT going to be ok! We are getting drug off one by one and we have no fucking idea why!"

"It has to be a reason!" Amy yells frustratedly, "It has to be a point to all of this!"

"But what if it isn't!" Kimberly challenges Amy's words and she looks at her. "Newsflash Amy, everything can't be explained! Maybe these are just sick people interested in mass kidnapping and slow torture! Maybe we were chosen randomly! Maybe it's just our time to die!" Tears roll down Kimberly's cheeks, but she doesn't react to them. I cry to myself, not knowing what to think or who to believe.

"Fuck this! I'm not dying like this! I didn't finally get where I wanted to be in life just to be killed randomly by some maniac!" Brandi has an outburst, looking like she's talking more to herself than to any of us.

"Brandi, we're fucked, just face it!" CeCe exclaims. Brandi looks over at her.

"No! You may be fucked, but I'm not!" She turns her attention towards Amy, "I wasn't done with my confession." We all look at Brandi and she takes a deep breath. "Well, when my stepson and I first started sleeping together, we couldn't stay away from each other. We were reckless and impulsive, and… I got pregnant." Most of our faces go from terrified to shocked. Cynthia makes the most disgusted face I've ever seen.

"You are despicable! How could you do something like that?" Brandi looks at her as if she wants to respond with a snappy comeback, but the seriousness of the situation stops her from going there. Instead, she ignores her, "Anyway, I ended up getting an abortion. I'd never been pregnant before, so I didn't realize I was until I was about three months pregnant. I got it taken care of as soon as I found out."

"You are a terrible person," Cynthia spews out after Brandi's story, continuing down her judgmental path. "For you to pay someone to suck that little precious soul out of you is literally pure evil!" Brandi frowns at her.

"I've lost one, too," CeCe chimes in. She humps her shoulders as if it's no big deal.

"Wait a minute, so you've been pregnant, too?" Amy asks, staring at CeCe. CeCe shakes her head yes quickly, like it's something that she no longer wants to talk about. Amy looks at Kimberly and Kimberly turns away immediately. My brain starts thinking a single thought over and over again. *I've been pregnant before as well.*

"Who here has been pregnant before?" Amy asks the room. All of the women admit to it except for Vicki. Amy turns her attention towards her, "Vicki, what about you?" Vicki still has her hands covering her face, wrapping up her crying. She sits up where she is and turns towards us. She stares at Amy for a second before eventually nodding her head yes. She looks down in shame right after.

"Wait a minute, so all of us have been pregnant before?" I question the room, even though I already heard every woman in here say that they have.

"Yeah. I guess we finally found something that we all have in common." CeCe exclaims.

"Ok… wow…" Amy blurts out, trying to process the information she just received. She stares in the distance for a minute, thinking about her next words. "So, I guess the follow-up question would have to be if you went through with your pregnancies or not?"

"I've already told you, I didn't. I couldn't have a baby with Junior for obvious reasons," Brandi answers first.

"And I already mentioned that I lost mine," CeCe adds quickly. She acts uncomfortable about the subject, as if the story behind it is something that she really doesn't want to talk about. Amy looks in my direction and I swallow hard with nervousness. *Even though I admitted to being pregnant before, I'm still not ready to tell anyone what happened.*

"I got an abortion." Vicki speaks up and Amy turns her attention from me to her. *Thank God.* "I got pregnant by Mr. Turner, and he paid for me to get rid of it when I was two months pregnant. There isn't a day that goes by when I don't think about my baby. I could have raised it by myself and no one would've ever known he was the father." Vicki stares at Amy blankly and the room gets quiet. No one knows what to say. *What can we say?*

"What about you, Amy? You've asked a lot of questions, but haven't answered any. What happened with your pregnancy?" CeCe turns the tables on Amy and she swallows hard. She glances at Kimberly again and I notice it. *Why does she keep looking at her?*

"Well…" Amy sighs. She stares at Kimberly again. Kimberly nods her head yes quickly before looking away. "Well, Kimberly and I were in a relationship." Brandi gasps before looking at Cynthia with perky ears. She knows that she can't wait to judge their lesbian situation. Cynthia doesn't say anything and Brandi looks shocked. *I'm honestly shocked, too.*

"Things were pretty serious between her and I, so serious in fact that we decided to start a family." She looks around at all of us nervously as her uncomfortableness grows. She takes a long blink before she continues, "We couldn't decide who would have the baby so we decided that we would both get pregnant, and if we timed everything right, we could raise them like they were twins. Plus, they'd be biological siblings because they'd have the same father, and they'd each have a part of us because we would both be their mothers." Her eyes tear up to match Kimberly's already wet eyes. Amy stares at her until she returns the glare.

"So, we went online and searched for the perfect guy for months to father our children, and we finally found one… John." Amy rolls her eyes when his name leaves her lips, "John was the perfect male specimen. He was tall, athletic, handsome, had perfect genes, and he passed his STD test with flying colors. Plus, we both have been with men before, and he checked out very well in the sexual department. So, after trying only once, we both got pregnant. We couldn't believe it! Happily ever after, right?... Wrong." Kimberly sighs as if Amy's about to tell a part of the story that she doesn't like. She gives Amy a weird look and Amy returns it, "Things were going great at first. John was supposed to impregnate us and go on his merry little way, but then he and Kimberly started talking, and all of a sudden, they were friends." Her voice gets angry, "Then, before I knew it, like four months into our pregnancies or so, she told me that she was leaving me for him! Could you believe it? The moment we decide to have a family and fully commit to one another, she decides she wants to go full hetero!" Kimberly looks shocked by her words.

"Before you knew it?! Don't try to make it seem like you weren't expecting that to happen! You stopped loving me!"

"I never stopped loving you!" Amy responds to Kimberly's statement quickly, "I just had other shit going on and I couldn't be up your ass every second of the day!"

"Just cut the shit, Amy! You loved your little bullshit website more than you loved me! I mean, come on! We were about to have a family!" Amy looks taken aback.

"I know! I was pregnant, too!"

"Ladies!" I interrupt them. I can't deal with any more of their yelling, "What happened to your babies?" They both make shamed faces as new tears surface in their eyes.

Amy looks down at her hands, "Well, when she left me like she did, I was devastated. I was pregnant with half of our twins by the guy that she chose to run off and leave me for… so… I got an abortion." She closes her eyes tightly, forcing her tears to trickle down her cheeks. I look over at Kimberly, waiting for her to answer the question as well.

"I- " She swallows hard, "I lost her when I was seven months pregnant, my baby girl." Amy's eyes get so big that her eyeballs look like they're going to pop out of her head.

"What?! What the hell do you mean you lost her?! Before you left me, you told me that you were getting an abortion! That was part of the reason why I got an abortion! I can't believe you fucking lied to me!" Amy breathes hard like she's about to have a panic attack. Kimberly buries her face in her hands and sobs loudly. Everyone else in the room looks at them uncomfortably.

"Well, that's why all relationships should be boy/girl. Look at how all of this confusion caused two innocent babies to be purposely conceived and then terribly murdered." Cynthia finally allows her judgmental words to join the conversation and Kimberly gets extremely offended.

"I didn't murder my child! I just said I lost her!"

"How?" Amy manages to ask through her tears. Kimberly looks at her before putting her head down again.

"John-" Kimberly shakes her head no as if she's trying to shake away an awful memory, "He got drunk one night and accused me of still sleeping with you. The argument got bad… really bad. He grabbed my arm and I tried to get away. I was near the top of the stairs. I snatched away from him forcefully, I-" She stops talking and covers her face again. She cries harder before finishing her statement, "I fell down the steps. I tumbled really violently.

As soon as I hit the floor at the bottom, I started to bleed

heavily. My baby died instantly." Her cries turn into sobs

so loud that she can barely finish her story, "My fall killed

my baby girl!"

CHAPTER SEVEN

Kimberly cries painfully after her last words. Amy's eyes go from furious to devastated. We all sit there in uncomfortable silence yet again. *That sounds like an awful way to lose a baby. I'm glad my situation wasn't that horrendous.*

"Why didn't you tell me?" Amy asks Kimberly, allowing more tears to fall right after her question. Kimberly quiets her crying and looks at her guiltily, wiping her tears away even though they're quickly being replaced by others.

"I don't know." She humps her shoulder lightly, "I was ashamed… embarrassed. I had already lied to you about getting an abortion, so I couldn't expect you to comfort me through losing my baby, even though you were the only person on this Earth that could have helped me get through that." Amy stares at Kinberly with concerned eyes. She looks as if she wants to know more, but doesn't inquire. They both look so broken-hearted that I start to feel their pain. The room gets very solemn. CeCe takes a deep breath before breaking the depressing silence.

"I was having a baby girl, too. She would have been three last month." CeCe gives a half smile to the thought, before letting her own sadness take over.

"Baby girl? So you lost your baby when you were further along, too?" Kimberly asks depressingly, bonding with CeCe over their similar and unbearable sounding subject. CeCe nods her head yes while looking down at her hands.

"Yup. I lost her when I was six months pregnant."

"So, what happened?" CeCe glances at me like she doesn't like my question, but she starts to answer it anyway.

"I…" she blows air out of her mouth as if she's about to say something major, "I had a problem before… a drug problem. I was addicted to prescription drugs."

Everyone looks surprised by the news, even though it's apparent that she has over-indulged in control substances at one time in her life or another. She takes another deep breath before continuing, "My best friend that I was talking about earlier that died, well, he knocked me up a while back. We would both get really high off of his mom's pain pills and have sex. We did it so much that I got pregnant." She shifts uncomfortably on the hard floor, "We were taking so many of his mom's pills that she almost instantly figured out what we were doing. She started locking up her medications, so we found a dealer and got even higher than before. I didn't even know I was pregnant," she humps her shoulders, "Hell, even if I did, it wouldn't have mattered. I was strung out, like big fucking time. I built up a tolerance after a while, so I started to take pills more often. Getting high became harder and harder for me to do-" she stares down at the floor, "So, I popped too many pills one day and overdosed. I was rushed to the hospital. I almost died. By the time I came to, they told me that I was six months pregnant, but she had died. I became fucking furious when I heard that! Like, how could I have been six months pregnant and my stomach wasn't even poking out?" She shakes her head, "I was in denial for a long time. I don't know, I guess it was easier than accepting the fact that my addiction killed my first child." CeCe finally shows remorse and a tear falls. She wipes it away hastily, staring embarrassingly at the corner furthest away from the group. Her eyes get big immediately before her mouth falls open.

"Hey, y'all? What the fuck happened to Vicki?"

***

All of our eyes quickly shoot towards the same corner and I almost urinate on myself. Vicki and her chain are gone as if they were never there! I feel myself having an anxiety attack, but I quickly try to control it. *Now is not the time to completely lose it, Jessica!*

"No! No... that's not right! It can't be!" Amy shakes her head in disbelief, "If they snatched her away, she would have screamed. I didn't hear anything- did you?" She looks at all of us quickly. We all shake our heads no immediately.

"It can't be, but it is! You told us that if we confessed our deepest, darkest secrets, then we would make it out of here alive!" Brandi screams at Amy and Amy shakes her head defensively.

"Hey! Don't fucking jump on me! I was merely suggesting solutions! I never guaranteed anything would work! I'm doing more than any of you! At least I'm coming up with something, instead of sitting here crying and waiting for my turn to be drug off to God knows where!"

"Maybe this is God," I blurt out to no one in particular. I stare at the spot where Vicki was sitting and take a deep breath. The ladies stop arguing and look at me. "None of you have brought it up once, but I know you've been thinking about it, because I have, too. What if this is the act of God, like purgatory or something?" Brandi shakes her head with a chuckle.

"Fuck that theory! I am responsible for my life, not some divine being! Everything that has gone right in my life has been because I applied myself! I worked hard! I created my own opportunities!" She breathes hard with her words, as if she's two seconds away from going mad. Her and I lock eyes before she lets out an ear shattering scream. We all watch in horror as her body slides rapidly towards the wall. Her lovely gown rips at the split once it gets caught on the uneven spots over and over again on the cement floor. Her body rests inches away from the velvet curtain, just like the others. She breathes fearfully before wiping her face speedily and sitting upright. She closes her eyes and takes deep breaths to center herself. She breathes out slowly one last time before turning around with a new demeanor to face us.

"Even though it's my turn to go, I'm not going to allow them the satisfaction of seeing me sweat. I've demanded respect my whole life, so I'll be damned if I stop doing that now just because I'm faced with death. I'm better than that." She attempts to fix her ripped gown over her legs. I stare at her expressionless. My body has gone numb. *I guess I've finally accepted the fact that I'm about to die as well.*

"Why is this happening?" Amy whispers to herself. She closes her eyes as if she's concentrating hard. "There has to be something… something I'm overlooking."

"Maybe you should consider Jessica's explanation. God is most definitely real." Cynthia chimes in and we all look at her.

"Don't tell me that you're a Christian," Brandi asks with a snicker, sounding low because she's so far away from the rest of us now. Cynthia narrows her eyes at her.

"Of course I am! My kids and I go to church to praise my Lord and Saviour every Sunday morning." She waves her hand to the sky and Brandi chuckles.

"Actually, that makes perfect sense for her to be a Christian," CeCe says, looking in Brandi's direction, "Christians are the most judgmental people I know. Do you know that when I finally decided to get help for my addiction, I went to a rehab facility that was run by a local Christian organization. Let's just say that those people were worse than the folks I've met out on the streets. I had to go somewhere else to get the help I needed."

"You never would have needed the help if you never would have started taking drugs in the first place." Everyone rolls their eyes at Cynthia's statement, including me. *Does she ever quit?*

"You know what, Cynthia? That's a great suggestion. I'm not sure why I never thought of it myself." CeCe speaks facetiously but Cynthia doesn't pick up on it.

"Well, Ms. Church Every Sunday, if you and your God are as close as you say you are, then why are you being held captive with us sinners, then?" Brandi's question catches Cynthia off guard, causing her to go from looking proud to embarrassed in a matter of seconds. We all stare at her. Our eyes look like spotlights shining brightly in her direction, "Ahh… not too quick to speak up if your words aren't being used to persecute someone else, I see."

CHAPTER EIGHT

Cynthia starts to say something, but she quickly stops herself. Instead, she sighs loudly and adjusts her old looking t-shirt to buy herself some time.

"I do have an excellent relationship with Jesus," she tries to sound confident, but her voice is too shaky for any of us to believe her, "So excellent in fact, that I can be one of his disciples." Brandi laughs hysterically at Cynthia's claims, making Cynthia look even more uneasy. She tries to ignore Brandi's obnoxious chuckles as she doubles down on what she's saying, "I can feel Jesus all of the time, hear him whenever he speaks, so that's probably why I'm here with you all. Maybe I'm supposed to be the voice of reason in this room of red... get you to see your wrongs before it's too late!" She sounds like a preacher towards the end of her spiel and CeCe laughs at her this time. Amy giggles, too.

"I call bullshit." Brandi continues to challenge Cynthia. Cynthia finally looks at Brandi with furious eyes.

"Oh, shut up, tramp! You think you know what you're talking about, but you have no fucking idea!"

"Ohh! I didn't know that talking like that was the Christian way!" Brandi smiles big after her words, loving the fact that she's finally able to get underneath Cynthia's skin. Cynthia's face turns red with anger.

"You ignorant whore! You will never be blessed! God isn't a joke, you blasphemous bitch!" She spits her words out aggressively, seeming to be a little too passionate about what she's saying. Brandi laughs again as if she's being tickled.

"Must I say it again? I'm beautiful, and married to a billionaire. What else is there?"

"Being a mother! You may have gotten pregnant before, but someone as filthy and whorish as you will never carry a child full term! Your womb has been rotted with the semen of sin!" CeCe shakes her head.

"Where do you get this shit? Sin semen?" CeCe chuckles after throwing her own question out there. Cynthia gawks at both CeCe and Brandi as if she's being double-teamed.

"I told you, I can hear my Lord and Saviour! This is what he wants me to tell you all today! Out of every woman in this room, I'm the only one that has birthed children! I've carried life inside of me three times-"

"Three?" Amy cuts Cynthia off with her own inquiry. Cynthia turns her attention towards her, "Did you just say you were pregnant three times?"

"That's right," Cynthia answers with her chest poked out.

"Ok. So, if you've been pregnant three times, then why is it that you only have two kids?" Cynthia looks taken aback, wondering how Amy knew that. They stare at each other for a second before Cynthia makes a face as if she's been exposed. Brandi's eyes get big after she realizes what Amy is talking about.

"Oh yeah… that's right! You did mention your kids earlier! You said that you had two boys!"

"Yeah, she did." CeCe takes over where Brandi left off, "So, what happened to the other baby?" Everyone gets quiet and looks in Cynthia's direction, waiting for her to explain herself. She doesn't start talking right away and Brandi takes advantage of her silence.

"I can't believe it! You've been sitting here judging all of us this entire time when you are a baby murderer, too?"

"I DIDN'T MURDER MY BABY!" Cynthia shouts so loudly that I jump from the extreme change of her voice. Sam and Kimberly jump, too. "I! … I JUST! …" Cynthia begins to cry once she realizes that she can no longer keep up her fake facade. She slumps her shoulders down with defeat almost immediately after her speechlessness. For the first time during this entire ordeal, Cynthia seems as flawed as every other woman in this room.

"'I… I just.'… Oh, shut up! You're a sinner, just like the rest of us!" Brandi mocks Cynthia before yelling at her nastily. I listen to her words and frown. *Her kicking Cynthia while she's down is very unbecoming of her.*

"Yes! Yes, I'm a sinner! One of the worst sinners actually!" Cynthia breaks down emotionally right before my eyes and I feel sorry for her. She's breathing so hard that I think she's going to have an asthma attack.

"Hey, Cynthia, just relax. It's ok-"

"No! It's not ok! I'm a terrible person and I deserve everything that I'm going through right now!" Saliva flies from her lips, landing all over her already dirty shirt. She foams at the mouth like a deranged animal and I cringe.

"How could I?! After having two other babies, how could I treat my third one so badly?!" She starts questioning herself in front of everyone. We all look confused, hoping that she'll give us more info about what she's ranting about. She stares blankly straight ahead and starts rocking side to side slightly. *I think her mind has officially cracked.*

"My baby! My poor baby!" She looks down as she mimics rocking an infant in her arms. Amy looks at her worriedly and decides to try to reel her back to reality.

"Cynthia? Cynthia, hey, it's ok." Cynthia doesn't react to Amy's words. I become worried about her as well. "Cynthia, look at me." Amy speaks louder, finally getting Cynthia's attention. She looks over at Amy slowly. Amy smiles warmly at her. "Cynthia? What happened to your third baby?" Cynthia's face goes from blank to distraught once she processes Amy's question. She looks back down at her empty arms.

"My husband. My husband left out one day and said he was going to the store. He promised he would be right back." Amy handles Cynthia like she's her therapist, analyzing her answer so that she can ask her a new question.

"What did he go to the store to get?"

Cynthia stares at Amy again, "A pregnancy test. I told him that I might be pregnant again and he volunteered to go and buy me one." Amy listens again, trying to choose her next words carefully.

"Well, were you able to take the test?" Cynthia's eyes well up with new tears. She stops rocking her fake baby and opens her arms, realizing that there's nothing inside of them.

"No! He never came back! He never came back!" She becomes irate again and Amy immediately tries to calm her back down. She talks soothingly to her until her hysteria becomes manageable.

"It's ok, Cynthia… it's ok, because you didn't need the test anyway, right? Evidently, you were pregnant." Cynthia nods her head at Amy as if she agrees. Amy hesitates before she asks her next question, afraid that Cynthia will get emotionally bent out of shape all over again. "So, after you discovered that you were pregnant, what did you do next?" Cynthia looks away from Amy and closes her eyes. She wants to have another outburst but she fights it. Instead, she looks back at Amy.

"I- I went on with life the best way that I could. I was terribly overwhelmed because my husband brought in most of the income. I had to take care of the boys, go to work, and pay the bills all by myself. I didn't have time to worry about being pregnant."

"So, you never made a doctor's appointment or anything to get you and the baby checked out?" Amy continues to question Cynthia in a caring tone. Cynthia nods her head yes quickly.

"I did! A couple of times! I- I just never made it to any of them. I became too stressed out with my new way of life. I fell behind on bills almost instantly, my husband changed his phone number so I couldn't contact him… I was just…" She stares at Amy as if she doesn't know what else to say. Amy gives her a look as if she understands.

"So, is it safe to assume that you lost your baby?" Cynthia listens to the question, but doesn't answer. She looks down at her empty hands again and sighs loudly.

"No. I didn't lose him. He was born when I was eight months pregnant. He was a healthy looking baby boy." She grins at the thought of his little face, before looking mortified right after, "I had him in my car in the middle of the night, took one look at him, and then threw him in a dumpster."

CHAPTER NINE

Amy looks horrified after hearing Cynthia's confession and we all follow suit. The room gets quiet with surprise. Everyone remains shocked for a while, not sure of what to say next. Cynthia takes a deep breath before reluctantly continuing.

"So yeah, I've been accusing everyone of being a baby murder when in fact, I'm the real killer. It was a million other things I could have done. I could have taken him home with me, or left him on someone else's doorstep- fire station, police precinct, hospital, church. But... I didn't. I just looked at his sweet little face, wiggling around so healthy and lively, and I tossed him in the trash bin behind 7/11 like he was garbage. Then, I drove off before his cries could change my mind."

"You're sick! You know that? You're a sick person and you need help!" Kimberly speaks up in a distraught voice, becoming so upset that her body is shaking. Tears surface in her eyes after her words.

"I know, and I did get help. I turned to Jesus and he made it all better. He was my therapist, my healer, my everything, and he has since forgiven me, and that's all that matters." Cynthia's voice gains confidence again and I shake my head. *I can see now why she hides behind her faith. That's the only way she's able to live with herself.*

"Yeah, you should believe in God because you are nothing but the devil!" Kimberly adds angrily. I look in her direction, catching a glimpse of Brandi still sitting in the same spot she was in after sliding 20 or so feet across the floor. She stares at the curtain with a horrified expression as if she can hear something that the rest of us can't. Just then, the curtain starts to move weirdly, morphing from a hanging drape into something that resembles a fleshy mass. It sucks her in at lightning speed and I gasp loudly.

"Did anyone see that?!" I question everyone in the room frantically. They look at me as if my loud outburst startled them. "Brandi!... She just…" Everyone turns their heads towards where Brandi was sitting and looks surprised to see her no longer there.

"Jessica, what did you see?!" Amy asks me immediately. I swallow hard at her curiousness. *Did I really see what I thought I saw, or have I officially lost my damn mind?* I question my sanity before answering her. I think about Amy's inquiry for a few more seconds, deciding to tell her exactly what my eyes assumed were real.

"She- she was just sitting there, staring at the curtain like… I don't know… like it was talking to her or something. But then-" *I pause. I'm going to sound crazy as hell for this next part, but it is what I saw,* "But then, the curtain turned into this thing that moved like human flesh, and she was sucked in it so quickly, almost like-" I search my brain for the words that I'm looking for. Amy sighs as if she's found them for me.

"Almost like she was being aborted?" Amy throws out an ending to my story and I look at her terrifiedly. *I didn't think of it that way, but now that she mentions it, that's exactly what it looked like.*

"Yeah. Something like that." I agree with Amy as she sighs again.

"That makes no sense," CeCe finally says in a low tone, sounding like she believes what I said more than she's willing to admit.

I hump my shoulders, "Well, that's what I saw."

"But I don't understand." Kimberly's voice shakes through her statement. Amy looks at her.

"I think I do. I'm finally starting to figure it out. I think I know why we're here," Amy declares. We all look at her, desperate for some sort of explanation at this point. She makes eye contact with every woman that remains in the room. She takes a deep breath, preparing herself for how unrealistic her words are about to sound, "We've all been pregnant before, but our babies didn't make it for one reason or another. Either we've paid someone to kill them, lost them through a careless act, or flat out murdered them ourselves," she glances at Cynthia, "but either way, our babies didn't survive." She sighs loudly while looking down at her hands. "I don't know if this is the act of God, or the government, or... I don't know, but I'm almost sure that we're here to pay for what we've done to our unborn."

***

We all sit in awkward silence wanting to protest her words, but on what grounds? The facts surrounding this situation thus far is what led her right to her conclusion, and I can't say that I disagree.

"But why like this? Why in this fashion?" I ask her. She looks at me with moist eyes, as if she's trying very hard to fight back her tears.

"I'm not sure. There are a lot of holes in my explanation, but we're running out of TIME!" Amy shouts out her last word as her body slides swiftly across the floor. Kimberly screams out for her as she nears the velvet curtain. Amy lays there for a second, not reacting to what just happened to her at all. She wipes her eyes before sitting up and looking in our direction. She takes a few deep breaths before immediately going into survival mode, "Ok ladies, since I'm on borrowed time, we have to figure out what's going on right now! I'm going to talk this out with you guys as long as I can before they take me away." Kimberly cries hard after Amy's words, reaching her arms out for her. She cries so hard that tears begin to leave my eyes, too.

"Amy, I'm so sorry about everything! I hate that I lied to you and I've never stopped loving you!" Kimberly begins to pour her heart out to Amy and Amy grins. Her tears roll down her face to match Kimberly's and mine.

"I know. I've never stopped loving you, either."

"Baby, I'm so sorry! I never should've left! I never should've broken up our family!" Kimberly cries hard again and Amy joins her. The other ladies start to cry, too. *This whole situation is overwhelmingly heartbreaking.*

"Ok, enough about that, we don't have much time," Amy says, trying her best to pull herself together enough to get back to the topic at hand. "So, what do we know?"

"We know that we're fucked!" CeCe reverts back to her favorite line, wiping her tears away with her hands. We all look at her before thinking the same thing ourselves.

"Well, besides us being pregnant before, I think I heard some of us say that we've been to the hospital before for some sort of traumatic experience. Maybe someone with access to the hospital records is responsible for this." Sam nods her head as if she agrees with Kimberly's comment. CeCe humps her shoulder as if it's a possibility. Cynthia shakes her head no.

"But, I've never been to the hospital for anything like that before. Not once." The wind leaves Kimberly's sail immediately as her suggestion goes out of the window. The room gets quiet again. We all seem to be struggling in the critical thinking department.

"Ok, how about this, insteading of talking about what we do know, let's talk about what we don't. Like, what are the questions that we need answers to?"

"Hell, everything." CeCe throws out. Amy sighs impatiently.

"More specific than that." CeCe thinks about Amy's statement for a few seconds before responding.

"Ok. Well... why us? I know several women living on the streets that get abortions all of the fucking time, so why us, huh? Or why now? I haven't even lived my fucking life yet! I just got completely clean and started a new fucking job, so why now, at this exact time?" CeCe gets upset with her questions. Her eyes well up with more tears before she continues, "Or why were the nine of us put together? Why is it that I needed to meet y'all before I met my maker? What's so fucking special about y'all?"

"Wait a minute! Rewind that back- you said the nine of us?" Amy interrupts CeCe's emotional outburst and she makes a confused face.

"Yeah, it's nine of us. Well... It was." CeCe shakes her head at our new reality. Amy's eyes get big as if she just realized something.

"Oh my gosh! It's nine of us! I can't believe that I didn't notice this before!" We all stare at her with intrigued faces, waiting to hear what she's so excited about all of a sudden. "It was nine women for nine months! And after thinking about it, I realize that we all lost our babies during different months of our pregnancies!" She looks at all of us from a distance, pausing for a second to gather some more of her thoughts, "I think that we are all being aborted from this room in the same order that we aborted our babies."

CHAPTER TEN

"Wait a minute… what?" Kimberly asks confusedly. Amy looks at her with wide eyes.

"Kim, baby, think about it! Think about everything we've heard from every woman in here! Vicki, who sat over there and said that she was messing with the married dude and got an abortion at two months! Brandi said she got hers at three months, and me, I got mine at four!" Kimberly listens to her ex carefully before finally understanding what she's getting at. I finally get it, too. *I guess I'll be the last one to go, then.*

"But none of this makes any sense-"

"You can say that again." CeCe cuts Kimberly off in agreeance while shaking her head. I shake mine, too.

"Well, I guess we now know the order we'll be taken away, then," Amy adds in a troubled tone.

"Right, but I don't remember anyone saying they lost their baby during their fifth month." Kimberly continues to talk it out with Amy. Sam raises her hand slowly and we all look in her direction.

"It was me, I lost my baby at five months." Our mouths fall open, completely blown away at Sam's ability to talk, "And I never got a chance to make my confession. I've been lying to everyone about everything."

***

We sit there, staring at Sam as if she is a stranger now. *I must admit, I didn't see this one coming.*

"Lying about everything?" Amy asks. Sam takes a deep breath and nods her head.

"Yes." Everyone pauses.

"Well, we definitely know that you were lying about the being mute thing, so what else do you have to come clean about?" CeCe questions Sam and they make eye contact. Sam eventually diverts her eyes away with embarrassment.

"The cabin situation… I mean, about the details. My friends and I were trapped after an avalanche, but they didn't die from eating old food, they actually died because… well…" Sam stops talking and closes her eyes. Tears begin to trickle down her cheeks and fall onto her white shirt. Amy becomes impatient again and speaks up.

"They died because of what? I'm running out of time here-"

"They died because I poisoned them!" Sam forces her words as if they hurt to come out. She lets out all of the air in her lungs after her confession. It seems like her saying that outloud for the first time gave her a sense of relief. Kimberly's eyes grow big with shock.

"I can't believe it! Another killer?!" Cynthia makes an offended face after Kimberly's words. She knows that statement was about her, but she doesn't say anything. Amy shakes her head in disbelief.

"Wow," Amy pauses, "So, why did you do it?" Sam runs her hands through her auburn hair. She grabs a strand and twists it around her finger.

"I thought I did it for survival purposes, but now that I really think about it, I'm realizing that it was more to it than that." She looks in Amy's direction, "I went to the cabin with my boyfriend, my best friend, and her boyfriend. Well, I can't necessarily call him my boyfriend… we had actually just broken up, but the trip was already planned, so we went together anyway." She takes a deep breath as she begins to relive those painful moments, "Once we got there, we started fighting almost instantly. I couldn't prove it, but I knew he was fucking with my best friend behind my back. I just knew it!" Sam gets furious all of a sudden, but continues with her story. "They both denied it, even though I knew they were lying. Her boyfriend knew it, too. He knew it, too." She talks as if she's trying to convince herself more than us. I question her mental health as she gets further into her story, "I was going to leave, but then all of that snow fell. We were stuck with each other, and that's when all hell broke loose."

"What do you mean?" CeCe inquires. Sam looks in her direction this time.

"They all started attacking me! Accusing me of things I wasn't doing, like sneaking and eating their food after they divvied up our individual rations! My ex even went as far as to take some of my food, saying that I ate some of his when I really didn't! So, I had to do something! I- I wasn't going to let them starve me!"

"So, that's why you poisoned them?" Amy jumps in Sam's story and she sighs. She glances in her direction again.

"Don't you understand, I had to do it! It was the only way that I was going to survive!" Amy shakes her head as if she understands, even though she's secretly repulsed by what she's hearing.

"And the baby? You said you've been pregnant before, so what happened with that?" Amy attempts to change the subject, throwing Sam off slightly. She looks down as if she's struggling to prepare her answer.

"Even though I did what I thought I had to do at the cabin, the whole situation made me sick to my stomach. That's the reason why I decided to act mute. I couldn't bring myself to talk about what happened with anyone. Every time I tried to, I would have a full blown panic attack. I just-, I couldn't." Amy makes an impatient face and Sam notices it. She clears her throat before finally answering the question at hand, "About a week after getting out of the hospital, I found out I was pregnant. I mean, I was floored! My ex and I were together for two years, and never once did we ever consider me getting pregnant. So, for me to pop up pregnant after we broke up and I- ...you know… did what I did…was insane! It didn't take long for my shock to turn into guilt, and my guilt to turn into depression. Despite all of that however, I kept telling myself that I could do it. I could raise my baby even though I killed it's father, but after months and months of me going back and forth with myself, I realized that I was lying about my capabilities. With the way that karma works, I'd die during childbirth or something." She shakes her head at the thought, "So, I started thinking. The hospital had me on pills that were a big no no for pregnant women. I had stopped taking them when I found out I was pregnant, but I started taking them again, even doubling up on doses sometimes. I didn't think it would work, but one day when I was five months pregnant, I miscarried right in the toilet.

Even though that's what I wanted, I still cried through the entire ordeal." She drops new tears as she thinks about the moment it happened, "I was so distraught, that it took me two days to flush it."

CHAPTER ELEVEN

Just when I thought I've heard it all, someone tells a sick tale that leaves me in awe. I can't judge anyone based on their decisions, though. *I have my own horrible story to confess.*

"Wow," Cynthia says, knowing that she has no right to criticize anyone in this room anymore. Everyone gets quiet again. Kimberly stares helplessly at Amy.

"None of these stories are helping you though, Amy! I wish I knew how to save you!" Amy listens to Kimberly's painful words and smiles lovingly at her. They both silently cry as they fall heart first into each other's gaze.

"Shit! I mean, even though we have an idea of what's going on here, we still have no answers to the real fucking questions! Like, why us, and who the fuck is doing this!" CeCe gets irate again. Sam is the only person standing in between her and her destiny and she's not too happy about it.

"This has to be supernatural," I admit, referring to what I saw happen to Brandi a few moments ago. CeCe glances at me like she wants to protest but she would have no proof to back up her argument.

"She's so beautiful," Amy says in a low tone. We all look over at her and see her gawking at the velvet curtain.

"Baby, who is?" Kimberly asks curiously. Amy doesn't react to Kimberly's question at all. Instead, she continues to stare at the drape, almost as if she's hypnotized by it.

"Amy!" CeCe yells loudly, trying to get her attention. Amy still doesn't respond and we all become worried.

"Oh my God! What the hell is wrong with her?!" Kimberly cries out hysterically. Cynthia shakes her head with a smile.

"God's got her."

"Oh, bullshit!" CeCe shoots Cynthia's explanation down before it leaves her lips fully. Cynthia stares at CeCe with a very peaceful expression.

"You'll see. You'll see when it's your turn." Cynthia smiles at CeCe after her words, which takes CeCe over the edge. She angrily tries to get to Cynthia but her chain stops her from moving more than a few inches. Cynthia smiles even bigger, making her look sadistic. Chill bumps form on every inch of my body. *This whole situation is getting creepy as hell!*

"Yes… I'm ready." We hear Amy speaking again and we all turn to look at her. She talks to an unknown presence, acting as if she's forgotten about the rest of us entrapped in this place with her. The portion of the curtain sitting directly in front of her starts to wave as if someone has opened a window behind it. It moves a little more, ruffling faster after every second that passes.

"Ready for what?!" Kimberly asks another question, even though she knows it's going to fall on deaf ears. The curtain moves so swiftly that we don't notice the exact moment that it happens. The exact moment that the velvet material turns into living, slippery, blood tinged flesh. The exact moment that the chain around Amy's leg turns into a long, throbbing umbilical cord. Or the exact moment when the huge, hanging area of flesh opens and swallows Amy whole like she is a piece of chewed up food in someone's mouth. Even though we don't notice every exact moment, we still see it all, being completely uncertain of what 'it all' is.

"AHHH!" Kimberly shrieks in terror at the precise moment that Amy disappears. We all stare at the spot where the fleshy mass was again, completely taken aback at how quickly it turned back into a velvet drape. It hangs there so peacefully that I have to ask myself, *did I really just see what I'm almost sure I just saw?*

"What the hell?" Sam asks the air. She cries shocked tears while her mouth hangs open.

"You all saw that, right?... Right?!" Kimberly looks around at all of us frantically. No one answers her right away and she gets frustrated, "I'm not fucking crazy! I know what I saw!"

"I told you," I comment in a low tone. I'm almost speechless by the events that have just taken place, "I saw the same thing happen to Brandi. It's like we're in a big ass womb or something." Everyone looks around at the room again as if what I said just added a new level of creepy to an already eerie situation.

"But that makes no..." CeCe speaks quietly as her eyes scan the room. She still wants to disagree with my explanation, but not even she can deny what she just witnessed.

"Amy was right, we're being aborted." Sam's eyes never leave the spot where Amy was sitting. Kimberly looks at her after her words.

"Aborted to where?" Kimberly asks fearfully. Sam rolls her head slowly in Kimberly's direction. Their eyes finally meet and Sam takes a deep breath.

"I have no idea, but I'm next in line to find out."

CHAPTER TWELVE

Sam takes a deep breath as if she's trying her best to come to terms with her fate. I secretly start to admire her bravery. *I don't know if I'll be able to hold it together when my time comes.*

"I don't understand. I really don't understand." CeCe still can't wrap her head around everything that's happening. She stares around the room one last time.

"God is over all of this. What's so hard to understand about that?" Cynthia continues her religious talk even though she knows it's going to rub CeCe the wrong way. CeCe doesn't even acknowledge Cynthia this time. *I don't blame her.*

"Were we even kidnapped, then?" Kimberly asks no one in particular. I think about her question before attempting to answer. *How else would we have gotten here?*

"What do you mean?" I inquire shortly after her question. Kimberly humps her shoulders as if she's not even sure what she means.

"I think what I'm trying to say is that I know what I saw, and I know how impossible what's been going on is to happen under normal circumstances. So, have we been kidnapped, drugged, and taken somewhere, or are we-"

"Don't you say it!" CeCe cuts Kimberly off abruptly. Kimberly sighs and closes her eyes. She honestly didn't want to say it, either, even though it's definitely a possibility. *What if we are no longer alive?*

"I mean, what else can this be? We're either drugged or dead. What else can explain what's been going on here?" Sam states, constantly staring at the area where Amy was sucked up by the curtain. CeCe sighs and tries to think of another explanation quickly.

"Maybe we were abducted by aliens." CeCe blurts out the first idea that pops in her head. We all stare at her like that's the most ridiculous thing we've ever heard, *as if a curtain turning into flesh isn't just as ridiculous.* She reads our facial expressions and gets offended, "Seriously! Just think about it! We were snatched up without any knowledge of the event, and then we woke up somewhere strange with shit happening that is not of this Earth!" I nod my head at her explanation. I can kind of agree with her on that one. *This situation does sound like a scenario on one of those alien shows on the Discovery channel.* Cynthia chuckles after CeCe's theory.

"There is no such a thing as aliens."

"But there's such a thing as a sky daddy chained to a cross?" CeCe snaps back at Cynthia's statement to discredit her opinion. They stare at each other as if their chains are the only things that are stopping them from getting physical with one another. Sam shakes her head at both of them.

"Even with all of this craziness going on, you two still can't act civilized?" She shakes her head again. "I'm next to be snatched up and taken, just like all of us eventually will be, and you two won't-" Sam stops talking once her body gets yanked across the room by her ankle. She slides swiftly until she nears her portion of the velvet curtain.

"Sam! Are you ok?!" Kimberly yells out. Sam's face looks unbothered when she sits up to face us.

"I'm fine," she answers speedily. She checks a fresh scratch on her arm that she got while sliding across the uneven floor and wipes the small amount of blood away with her hand. "I deserve this. I've killed several people, and it's time for me to pay for what I've done." Sam speaks to us calmly, even though tears are in her eyes. I can tell that she's tired of carrying her burdens around. The guilt she feels appears to be too heavy for her shoulders.

The room gets quiet again. With almost half of us gone, the place seems bigger than before. I look at the remaining four women and sigh to myself. *I know each one of their stories in detail, but I still have yet to say anything about my own. Just in case there is a heaven and a hell, maybe I should clear my conscience before I die.*

"Umm…" I start. I clear my throat and the other women look towards me. My palms get sweaty and I wipe them on my yoga pants, "I seem to have been so curious about everyone else's stories, that I've managed to neglect my own." I let out a nervous chuckle. No one else's facial expression changes, making my artificial smile fade away quickly.

"That's by design, I'm sure," CeCe throws out, seeing right through me quickly. I look at her before looking down and humping my shoulders. I don't reply to her comment so she continues, "After Amy figured out the order that we will be taken, the process of elimination pointed to you being the last to go. Not only that, but you never said one thing about what happened to your baby. And if you're ninth for nine months, then it has to be one hell of a story." CeCe talks to me like she's pretty much figured me out. I look down again. *She's definitely not too far off.*

"Please don't tell me you threw your baby away, too?" Kimberly blurts out, sounding like she can't handle another murderer in her midst. I shake my head no quickly.

"I would never do anything like that!" I rebut defensively. Kimberly makes a relieved face while Cynthia makes an embarrassed one.

"Ok then... if you didn't murder your baby, then what happened to it?"

"Him." I correct CeCe rapidly, before looking down in shame immediately thereafter. I take a deep breath and close my eyes. *Here I go.* "I met him in high school. He was the captain of the basketball team and I was the nerd in the back." I smile slightly as I remember my innocent years, "It was a million girls waiting for him to ask them to prom, but for some strange reason, he asked me. At first I said no, thinking that he was playing some sort of prank on me, but it turned out that he was being genuine." I pause to take a deep breath. *That was the last time I remember him and I being truly happy.* "I was obsessed with him, mainly because my self-esteem was at zero back then. He was gorgeous and popular and I was… well… me." I hump my shoulders and notice everyone's eyes staring at me impatiently. I sigh to myself. *I can't believe I'm about to entrust some of my most hurtful memories with women that I barely even know.* I clear my throat again before I continue, "He started cheating on me after our first year of college. When I caught him, I was completely devastated. He apologized and said it would never happen again, so I believed him and took him back. A few times of me finding strange looking underwear and several incriminating text messages later, it became evident that he was lying to me. He was never going to stop cheating." My eyes tear up before I can go into the next part of my story. *Those years that followed almost destroyed me.* "After confronting him about it for the umpteenth time, he finally just came out and said that if I wasn't going to leave him for cheating, then I need to just shut up about it. My heart sank when those words left his lips, and I wanted to leave him so badly, but I loved him so fucking much… so… I stayed." CeCe shakes her head at my weakness once we lock eyes. I look away from her gaze embarrassingly, "Staying was the worst thing I could've done. He lost all respect for me after that. It went from him trying to hide the cheating to him constantly being seen running around town with other women, even bringing them to our home! He was getting completely out of control!" I get angry when I have a flashback of him getting caught with his pants down in our garage, "So I had to do something! Something to make him slow down…" I try to validate my actions before I reveal to them what I did. Kimberly narrows her eyes at me.

"Don't tell me that you got pregnant on purpose to keep him?" I sigh at her question before looking at her shamefully.

"Yeah. I lied to my ex-boyfriend about being on birth control so that I could trap him with a baby."

CHAPTER THIRTEEN

"Ok, and then what?" CeCe asks, hoping that I'll reach the end of my long confession soon. I glance in her direction before going back into my story.

"Then, things became okay for a while. That seemed to do the trick and put an end to his cheating, and we started making the normal plans that first time parents make. It wasn't until I went through his phone one night when I was almost nine months pregnant that I realized that he was still a no good cheater, and that wasn't even the shocking part!" Tears run down my face as I start to feel the pain that I felt back then all over again, "His new conquest was a man! I couldn't fucking believe it!"

"Whoa," Kimberly says with her mouth wide open. My tears stream constantly down my cheeks as my emotions get the best of me. "So, what did you do?" I wipe my tears with the back of my hands. I hesitate because I really don't want to answer the question. I need to, though. *It's time to get it all out in the open.*

"While reading the messages, I found out where they were supposed to be meeting the next night and I showed up to where they were. It was a motel on the other side of town that was a known spot for homosexual activity. I talked the guy at the front desk into giving me a key to the room they were in. Then, with my camera rolling, I busted in the door and caught him in a very compromising position. My timing was perfect. The footage I had was enough to ruin his life… so, that's what I did." I take a deep breath. *I'm not too proud of myself for what happened next,* "I uploaded it straight to my Facebook page. His family, friends, and old teammates saw it. In a few hours, the video had been shared almost a thousand times. It circulated quickly. He was more well-known than I thought." I wipe my eyes with the back of my hand again, "After I recorded them, I hurried from the motel room and sped home. I expected him to follow me so that we could argue about what I just did, but he never showed up. By the next morning, I felt like I went too far with the video thing so I went on Facebook to take it down. It was too late, though. It was already watched thousands of times and people had already copied the video, so even after I deleted it, it was still being posted and watched by other people online. It was crazy."

"This is a good story and all, but when are you going to get to the important part?" CeCe asks, getting irritated by my longwindedness. I sigh at her words. *I needed to give them as much backstory as possible so that I*

wouldn't seem like the bad guy.

"Well, to make a long story short, I got a call from his parents. Evidently, after I posted the video online and tagged him in it, he started to get a bunch of calls and texts from different people questioning or ridiculing him. Details are unclear about where the gun came from, but right there, in the motel bathroom, he shot himself in the head. Just one shot, and he was gone." I close my eyes as I remember him and what his smile looked like. My heart instantly aches for the pain I put his family through. His loved ones still haven't forgiven me.

The feeling of vocally crying creeps up my throat, but I fight it in order to finish my story. "I went into labor a week and a half later, and the doctors realized quickly that there was something wrong. Apparently, he was sleeping with that guy unprotected for a long time," I put my hands over my face, preparing myself to say something that I've never said out loud before, "And I found out that I contracted Syphilis and HIV from him and I didn't even know it!"

***

Everyone looks shocked as I cry audibly in my hands. *I can't believe that I just admitted that I'm HIV positive. That was a secret that I swore I would take to the grave.*

"Oh my God, so your baby was infected, too?" Kimberly asks, looking as if she feels sorry for me. I nod my head yes slightly.

"There was nothing they could do for him. He didn't have a heartbeat. He was stillborn." The room gets quiet as everyone tries to absorb what I just told them. I cry a little longer, remembering the funeral that I had to have for my precious baby boy. *He didn't deserve that. I should have left his father a long time ago.*

"Well," CeCe says, causing me to look over at her. She stares in the direction of Sam, and I follow her eyes. Sam is no longer there and I sigh loudly. CeCe turns her attention towards me, "I guess it's finally my turn."

Her and I stare at each other as if our eyes are having a deep conversation. Cynthia and Kimberly finally notice Sam's missing body, but they don't act shocked about it. We finally know why we're here, and we know exactly how things will end up for us. We just don't know what's on the other side of the curtain, which is the biggest question of them all.

The room is so quiet that it's almost peaceful. We all take some time to look within ourselves, reflecting on life as we know it. CeCe cries to herself silently and I notice it. I know exactly why she's crying. *The rest of us will be in her shoes very soon.*

"Fuck this! I'm not about to sit here and wait to slide across this hard floor! I can crawl over there myself," CeCe exclaims, turning her body around to move towards the velvet drape. The chain yanks her suddenly, causing her to fall weirdly on the hard surface and slide towards the curtain. "OUCH!" She yells out once her body finally rests near the drape. She sits up slowly and grabs her arm. "My fucking arm is broken!" she screams loudly. She tries to move it, but winces whenever she does. "Fuck you, you fucking bitch!" She screams at the curtain, kicking at it as if she can hurt it. It swings slowly with the wind from her feet.

"I wouldn't do that if I were you," Kimberly warns with a frightened face. CeCe ignores her as she kicks at the drape harder. "CeCe! Don't- AHH!" Kimberly starts shrieking loudly and we all look over at her immediately. Her body slides towards the curtain as well and my eyes get big. *Two women taken at once? That's never happened before!*

"What! Why is this happening?!" Kimberly cries out after she finishes sliding. CeCe stares in her direction as if it's her fault.

"I have no idea," I answer, completely taken aback by both women facing their parts of the curtain at the same time. Kimberly cries so loud that Cynthia covers her ears.

"Kimberly, stop all of that crying! Don't give whoever is doing this the satisfaction!" CeCe yells to her. Kimberly tries to control herself, taking her hysterical weeping down to a whimper. She sniffs a few more times before turning to face CeCe.

"CeCe, why the both of us? Why do you think we're being taken together?" Kimberly asks her in an innocent voice. She sounds so helpless and scared, sort of like she doesn't deserve this. I guess she actually doesn't.

Out of everyone else here, her story was the only one that didn't result in her baby dying because of an awful decision that she made.

CeCe sighs at her question before facing Kimberly as well. She stares at her helplessly, not knowing exactly what to say. They stare at each other for a while with no words spoken. The room gets quiet again. Cynthia starts praying and I decide to as well. *At this point, asking for forgiveness doesn't sound like a bad idea.*

"Oh my gosh! Do you hear that?" Kimberly asks, turning to look at the velvet curtain quickly. CeCe's ears perk up as if she can hear it as well.

"I couldn't at first, but now I do. What the hell is that?" CeCe and Kimberly stare at each other. The room goes silent as I try to figure out what they're talking about. *I can't hear anything.*

"It… It sounds like people. Like people talking," Kimberly adds, moving her ear closer to the drape.

"People talking? About what?" I ask in a desperate tone. She listens a little while longer before attempting to answer my question.

"I'm not sure, really. Babies I think. I think I heard the word, twins."

"You, too?" CeCe asks Kimberly. She glances at her after listening to her part of the curtain, "I heard someone say twins as well."

"Twins?" I say with a confused expression. "Why would people on the other side of the curtain be talking about twins?"

"Look at the light," Kimberly speaks calmly, completely ignoring my inquiries. She stares at the curtain as it starts to wave lightly. I swallow hard with fear. *That's exactly what happened before the hanging velvet turned into flesh and Amy was taken!*

"Who… Who is she?" CeCe asks in a frightened voice. Both her and Kimberly's eyes are locked on to their part of the curtain as if they can't turn away. I glance in both of their directions, but I don't see anyone. *Why is it that every time someone is taken, they can see things that others can't?*

"Aphrodite?" Kimberly questions someone, but not any of us in the room. I listen to the name that she says and draws a blank almost instantly. *I've heard of Aphrodite, but who is she?*

CHAPTER FOURTEEN

CeCe slides away first, disappearing into the fleshy mouth of what used to be a velvet curtain. She doesn't seem to react to it at all, as if her emotions have been turned off. Kimberly is swept away shortly thereafter, making a face of overwhelmingly emotional bliss. I notice that each woman has a different facial expression when they are being taken and I get confused. *Did they all see the same thing when it was their time to go, or were each one of them shown something different?*

"Well, it looks like it's just you and me," Cynthia says comfortably, causing me to make an unpleasant face at her. She notices it immediately and shakes her head.

"You don't have to believe what I believe, but that doesn't change the fact that it's the truth." I listen to her words and roll my eyes. I definitely believe in a higher power, I just don't believe that it'll protect her after what she did to her newborn child. I turn away from her, trying to give her the hint that I'm no longer interested in the things that she's saying. She begins to talk to me again anyway.

"Have you asked *him* for forgiveness yet?" I become annoyed by her question. I've never wished for anyone to be taken until now. *Isn't it her time to go already?* "I'm serious. You know-"

"Listen, Cynthia. I'm getting really tired of you, your criticisms, and your fake beliefs! You don't really believe in God that much, you're just hiding behind him out of fear that what you did has earned you a one way ticket straight to hell! Well, newsflash Cynthia! It did!" She looks shocked by me suddenly blowing up at her. She gets

furious at my words, letting me know that I've struck the

nail right on the head.

"Say whatever you want about me! I know my God

will save me! You're just mad because you caught the gay

man's disease!" She throws my confession in my face,

making me angry immediately. She smirks after she

realizes that she got under my skin. "You having sex out of

wedlock killed your baby. A child being born in sin is the

devil's dinner!" Her words strike a nerve in me and I see

red. I scramble towards her, only moving a few inches in

her direction because of the chain on my ankle. She

chuckles at my actions, "The truth hurts, doesn't it?" I

begin to cry. I thought I was over my baby dying, at least

that's what I've been telling myself for the past two years.

It took for me to go through this experience to realize that

I'm nowhere near done grieving over his untimely death, him or his dad's, and I probably never will be.

I cover my face and fill my hands with salty tears. I cry so hard that it burns my chest. I can't believe the only man I've ever been with volunteered to leave me by myself in the land of the living. He left me to bury a child that perished from his infidelities.

I cover my face until I hear Cynthia start to move. I look up and see her bodying sliding awkwardly across the floor. Her plus size build makes for an unpleasant travel across the rigid concrete. Her skin is red with welts when she sits up.

"Ouch!" She groans, pulling down her shirt that rolled up while she was sliding. She checks a few of her new wounds before staring straight ahead at the curtain. She clears her throat, "I'm ready, Lord! I know that you will take care of my boys while you lead me to the afterlife!" She speaks towards the drape loudly as if God himself is standing directly on the other side. She gets quiet as if she's waiting for a reply. After no one answers, I stare at her, waiting to see what silly antic she's going to try next. She makes a slightly nervous face before repeating herself, "Lord, I said I'm ready! I'm ready to go with you to the afterlife!" She gets quiet again, staring straight ahead in hopes of a reply. Again… nothing. I giggle to myself and she looks at me angrily.

"You may think this is a joke, but my God is real! He's going to personally take me by the hand and walk me to the other side… watch!" She speaks as if she's trying to convince herself more than me. I shake my head at her claims. *Everyone else was snatched away by a pulsating cord. I'm sure her experience will be no different.*

I refuse to comment on anything else she says and the room gets quiet. We sit there uncomfortably, impatiently waiting to see what happens next. I rock my body from side to side as my thoughts bounce between the other women that once inhabited this room to my dead boyfriend and son. I go through a rollercoaster of emotions. *I'm going to go crazy before my turn to be swallowed up even comes.*

"Wha- Wait a minute, you're not my God!" Cynthia screams, frightening me out of my depressing thoughts. She looks terrified and I perk up.

"Who isn't your God? What do you see?" Cynthia tries to crawl away, causing fear to rise up in my chest. *What if we really are being drug off to heaven or hell? Could that be the devil she's looking at right now?*

"Cynthia! Tell me what you see?!" I yell in an attempt to get her attention. She gets tired from her attempt to escape and lays down on her back.

"A woman!" She shouts back in my direction. I get baffled by her words quickly.

"A woman?" I repeat, questioning the air as my mind tries to process her answer. *What does she mean by 'a woman'?* I think for a few seconds more before I remember what Kimberly said.

"Is it Aphrodite?" I ask Cynthia, looking back in her direction. She stares at me with tears in her eyes as her body slides towards the fleshy mass and disappears into its opening.

CHAPTER FIFTEEN

I start to panic. *I'm all alone and it's officially my turn!*

"Aphrodite… Aphrodite… Who the hell is Aphrodite?" I talk out loud, trying to access the part of my brain that holds all of my college knowledge. *I know we talked about her in class, but which class was it?*

"Greek Mythology!" I shout out excitedly, "Aphrodite is a goddess in greek mythology!" I pat myself on the back before immediately feeling dumb for feeling so proud. Me figuring out who she is doesn't change the fact that I'm in this situation and I have no idea what's really going on here. Actually, identifying her creates more questions than answers. *Are these women really seeing a mythical character on their way out of this velvet capture?*

"I'll find out soon," I say to myself with a sigh. I rummage through my college class memories again. *What was Aphrodite the goddess of?*

"Love," is the first word that leaves my lips, "She was the goddess of love. What else?" I have a conversation with myself, secretly missing the other ladies that went from strangers to confidants in a matter of hours. *I'm sure they would have helped me figure this out.*

"Love, sex I think, and-" My eyes get big once my body swiftly slides towards the curtain. I try to stay on my butt, scared that if my bare back touches the floor, it'll get scratched by the uneven ground. I stop sliding once the curtain comes within inches of my feet. I finally get a close-up of the material and cringe up once I realize that it will be transforming into living tissue soon.

"But it looks like a regular drape," I whisper in disbelief. It seems heavy and retro, just like something I've seen at my grandparent's house once. I sit there barely moving, paying close attention to every little move the curtain makes. I'm so nervous about what's about to happen that I can pass out, even though I really don't want to. *I don't want to miss a single second of whatever is about to happen. I need to see what the other ladies saw.*

"My child…" I hear a faint whisper in the distance. I turn to look around the room, but besides me, it's empty. I sit still again, listening as hard as my ears will allow. I listen in silence until I hear the voice again.

"My child…"

"Yes?" I answer quickly. I look around again, feeling creeped out because I have no idea where the feminine voice is coming from. A bright light catches my attention directly in front of me. I stare at it in awe, watching it illuminate in front of the velvet drape. It's radiant and soothing, almost hypnotic. My facial expression softens as a shadowy figure appears in a transparent

fashion.

Her hourglass figure hovers directly in front of me,

but not in a threatening way. Her presence actually does the

opposite, it makes me feel safe and secure.

"My child…" she says again. My eyes tear up at the

overwhelming feeling that's created by her presence. I stare

at the outline of her with parted lips. "It is I who gave you

your heart shaped flower that is nestled between your

thighs. It is I who gave you your slippery canal that leads to

the chamber where lives are created. It is I who gave you

your warm womb that is used to protect your unborn. And

it is I who gave you the desire to use these gifts." My tears

fall from her words, and that's when I realize it. *Aphrodite

is the goddess of fertility.*

"All of these gifts I have given you my child, and

for one reason or another, they have become tainted. A

deed that cannot be undone." I feel a deep feeling of uncontrollable guilt and sadness. The situation with my ex did cause my body irreversible damage. *I'll never be able to have children again.*

"Don't fret, my child. I am not here to pass judgment, only to whisper these things to you to ensure that these events do not take place in your next life." I listen to her words with a heavy heart.

"Next life?" I ask in a pained voice. The curtain begins to transform behind her, but I barely notice it. Her ora smiles at me and I smile back. The peace I feel with her is greater than any serene moment I've ever experienced in my life. The grip on my leg feels different. I look down and notice that the chain has changed into an umbilical cord, contracting and throbbing with vital nutrients for a fetus. I can feel the nutrients pumping through my own veins, causing me to wonder for a second how any of this is even possible.

"Are you ready, my child?" I blink slowly at her question. I open my eyes and notice that the curtain in front of me is no more. The flesh has completely taken over the drape, and my eyes get big with fear. "Don't be afraid, my child. Everything is going to be ok now." I stare at the living tissue waiting for me to enter through it's small opening. The umbilical cord drags me in, making me want to scream, but I can't.

I slide through the tight, wet space and everything goes dark. I struggle to breathe, but I'm unable to. I panic instantly. I have no idea what's going on. I feel like I've been buried alive...

But then…

"Come on baby, push!" I hear a man's voice. I hear other voices as well, but his is the most clear. "There you go! You're doing great!" I look up and finally see light. It's at the end of a very narrow tunnel, but I can most definitely see it.

"The head is coming!" I hear a woman's voice say. I'm nearing the end of the tunnel. I think I'm finally about to exit it.

"Ahh!" I hear a scream when my head pops out. It's so bright in here that I can barely see a thing. Where am I? *It smells like a hospital here.*

"One more push, Mrs. Baker, and your baby will be yours to hold!" The woman speaking earlier says enthusiastically. I slide the rest of the way out of the canal. *The birth canal.*

My tiny body falls into someone's hands and I freak out. I start moving and kicking wildly. *What happened to my regular body?! Why am I so small?!*

"Congratulations, you two! It's a girl!" They lay me on a lady's chest and I freak out even more. I begin to cry loudly. The lady rubs my back as if she's trying to sooth me.

"It's ok, baby. It's ok. Mommy's here." I can't believe what I'm hearing! This can't be happening! *I was just a 26 year old woman a few seconds ago, so how am I a baby now?!*

Two nurses come over to retrieve me. They carry me over to the baby scale and lay me down. I cry nonstop. This is a fate worse than death. *I can't believe I've been born again.*

"Hey, did you hear about what happened to Jessica?" One nurse whispers to the other. She humps her shoulders quickly.

"Jessica, who?"

"You know Jessica! Jessica that we went to school with, that was dating Mr. MVP? She shared that video of him and that gay guy online that led to him killing himself?" The other nurse nods her head with her mouth open.

"Oh yeah! I remember that! Well, what happened to her?" The other nurse leans in closer, making sure that no one else can hear her gossiping.

"They found her body in a ditch near the gym downtown. Evidently, a car swerved off of the road and hit her, and they fled the scene. They cold-heartedly left her there to die. When they found her, she was still wearing her gym clothes. Poor thing." My heart sinks into the deepest part of my stomach when I learn about what happened to me. *I can't believe I died!* I cry even harder from the sad news, distracting the nurses from the conversation they are having about me.

"Aww...don't cry little one. We know you're cold. We'll be done with you in a few minutes, and then we'll give you back to your mommy." She smiles at me and wipes my forehead where I remember my wound being, "Welcome to the world, baby girl."